Scritch Scratch
We Have Nits

Written by
MIRIAM MOSS

Illustrated by
DELPHINE DURAND

ORCHARD

One day
a tiny insect,
no bigger than a small freckle,
climbed into Miss Calypso's classroom.

Nobody noticed...

Miss Calypso went on calling the register.
Ruby undid Polly's plait.
Joshua drew on Winston's back.
And Simon trimmed Karim's fringe.

crops

mops

drops

tops

2 + 2 =

The little louse had no wings.
But she had six strong legs
and she climbed straight into the Spelling Ship
hanging above Miss Calypso's head.

What a wonderful view!
Miss Calypso's cascading curls,
short crops, matted mops, tufty tops,
plaits, pigtails, ponytails...
even a frizzy wig on the plastic skeleton in the corner!

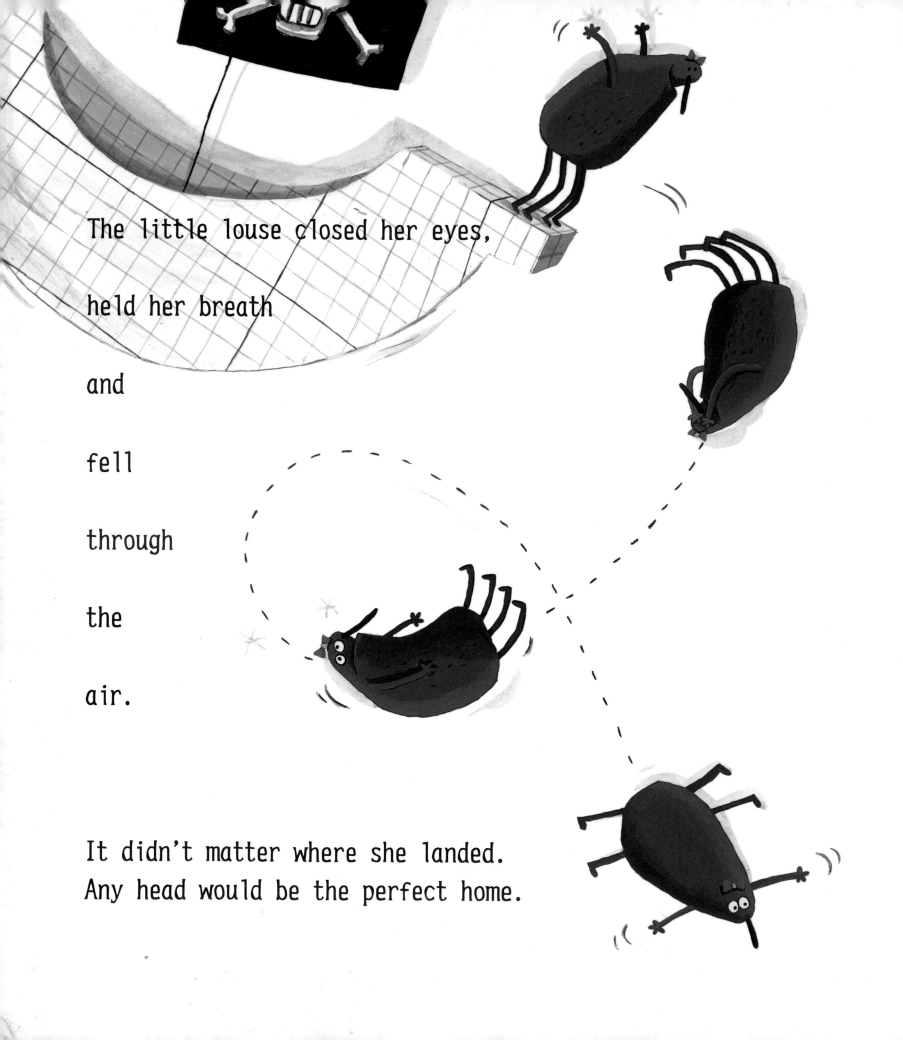

The little louse closed her eyes,

held her breath

and

fell

through

the

air.

It didn't matter where she landed.
Any head would be the perfect home.

And the perfect home she landed on was...

Miss Calypso!
The little louse got to work straight away,
sticking one tiny white egg to each
hair on Miss Calypso's head.

She hummed a happy tune.

Oh... No one knows from where I came,
A nit, a nibbler with no name,
But watch the teacher scritch and scratch,
When my creepy crawly family hatch.

Before long the creepy crawly family did hatch.
And they climbed into Miss Calypso's cascading curls.

Scritch Scratch went Miss Calypso,
                    praising Polly's pirate picture.

Scamper Scamper went the tiny headlice,
                    dancing down Polly's plait.

From

then on,

whenever

two

heads

touched,

lots of

little

headlice

moved

home!

Scritch Scratch went Polly,
playing with Ruby's hair.

Scamper Scamper went the headlice.

Scritch Scratch went Joshua,
drawing on Winston's back.

Scamper Scamper went the headlice.

Scritch Scratch went Simon,
trimming Karim's fringe.

Scamper Scamper went the headlice.

In no time at all,
the little lice had perfect homes
of their very own...

and that was when Mr Trout the Headmaster strode in!
"May I have a word, Miss Calypso?" he asked.
Miss Calypso agreed to meet him in the lunch hour
to discuss the scritching problem.

That night Mr Trout sent letters home
to all the parents.

Dear Parents,
Please comb special conditioner
through your children's hair
and make it so slippery
that all the headlice
slide into the bathwater
and float away

Once again Mr Trout went to see Miss Calypso. And there, in the little room where cups of tea are made, Mr Trout found himself offering to wash Miss Calypso's hair for her.

That night, while Mr Trout conditioned and combed Miss Calypso's hair, they fell in love. He fell in love with her cascading curls and she fell in love with his moustache.

So Mr Trout and Miss Calypso got married.
And now if you look into Mrs Trout's classroom—
what do you see?

Mrs Trout still calls the register.
Ruby still undoes Polly's plait.
Joshua still draws on Winston's back.
And Simon still trims Karim's fringe.

There's not a scritch or a scratch to be heard.
But...

there is a faint hum
from the classroom next door!

Oh... No one knows from where I came,
A nit, a nibbler with no name,
But watch the teacher scritch and scratch,
When my creepy crawly family hatch...

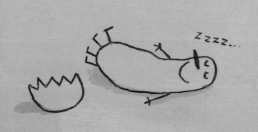

For Margot.
M.M.

For my family, my friends
and for Eunice.
D.D.

ORCHARD BOOKS
338 Euston Road
London NW1 3BH
Orchard Books Australia
Level 17/207 Kent Street, Sydney, NSW 2000
First published in 2001 by Orchard Books
First published in paperback in 2002
This edition published in 2012
ISBN 978 1 40831 958 1
Text © Miriam Moss 2001
Illustrations © Delphine Durand 2001
The rights of Miriam Moss to be identified as the author
and of Delphine Durand to be identified as the illustrator
of this work have been asserted by them in accordance with
the Copyright, Designs and Patents Act, 1988.
A CIP catalogue record for this book is available from the British Library.
10 9 8 7 6 5 4 3 2 1
Printed in China
Orchard Books is a division of Hachette Children's Books,
an Hachette UK company.
www.hachette.co.uk